←YOU CHOOSE→

WONDER WOMAN

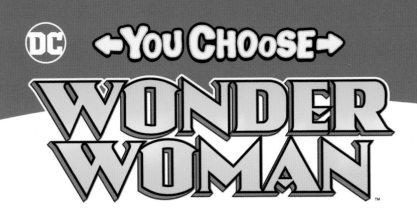

YOU CHOOSE

WONDER WOMAN™

THE CRYSTAL QUEST

written by
Laurie S. Sutton

illustrated by
Omar Lozano

Wonder Woman created by
William Moulton Marston

"What? No!" the hunters shout. "We're not prey!"

"Morgaine and I lured you into our trap and caught you in my rope snare," Wonder Woman says. "You are prey."

"We win," Morgaine says.

"All right. Release us and you are free to go," the leader says.

"Promise you won't hunt us again," Wonder Woman says.

"We promise," the hunters agree.

Wonder Woman lowers the men to the ground. As soon as she loosens the lasso, they run away into the jungle.

"What brave hunters," Morgaine scoffs.

"Come on, Morgaine," Wonder Woman says. "Let's get out of this habitat and find a way home."

THE END

To follow another path, turn to page 11.

Wonder Woman looks down at the pterodactyl nests. In her heart she cannot let Morgaine harm them, even if it means giving up the Zodiac Crystal. The stone is hard enough to hold onto as it is. The gem tugs and pulls against the Amazon's grip, trying to get to the second Zodiac stone.

"Very well, Morgaine, you may have the stone," Wonder Woman says. She lets go of the gem, and it shoots out of her hands. "But you have to catch it first!"

ZOOOOM!

The Zodiac Crystal flies past Morgaine in her dragon form. She tries to catch the gem, but her claws are too short.

SWOOOSH! Wonder Woman speeds past Morgaine in pursuit of the crystal.

"Arrgh!" Morgaine growls.

Morgaine returns to her human form and surrounds herself with a halo of magic.

Turn the page.

"Take me to the Zodiac Crystal," Morgaine whispers.

The magical energy around her glows and instantly transports her to the stone's location. Morgaine sees that she is outside a large pyramid. But she does not see the Leo Crystal or Wonder Woman.

"Has my magic failed me?" Morgaine wonders. She looks at the pyramid. It is similar to the ones in Egypt where the Leo Crystal was found inside the Great Sphinx. "No. My magic has served me perfectly. It has brought me to a *second* gem—inside the pyramid!"

Morgaine blasts the side of the pyramid with a bolt of magical energy, just like she did to the Great Sphinx.

BLAAAAM!

Meanwhile, Wonder Woman catches up to the Leo stone and arrives at the pyramid just in time to see Morgaine blow a hole in the side and step through it.

"I don't know how, but Morgaine seems to have found the location of the second Zodiac Crystal without using the Leo stone," Wonder Woman says. "But she does not have her hands on the second stone yet."

Gripping the Leo Crystal tightly, Wonder Woman lets the gem pull her into the pyramid as it seeks to connect with the second Zodiac Crystal. It takes her to a large chamber in the heart of the structure. There she finds Morgaine reaching for a large crystal carved in the shape of a scorpion.

Turn to page 58.

"I see that your golden lasso glows with a halo of powerful magic," Calculha says.

"It was forged by a god and is energized by the Fires of Hestia," Wonder Woman says.

"If I combine my magic with that of your lasso, I might be able to create an orb of protection large enough to contain the whole city," Calculha says.

"Your idea sounds daring, but I like it," Wonder Woman decides. "And the lasso has abilities that are just right for your plan. But first, we have to get high above the city."

WHOOSH!

Wonder Woman flies high into the sky. Calculha follows on his dragon. Soon they can see the whole city below them.

Wonder Woman starts to twirl the golden lasso. As it spins above her head, the loop starts to expand. **SWISH! SWISH! SWISH!** It grows larger and larger. Soon it is hundreds of feet wide. But Wonder Woman does not stop there.

"Get ready with that protection spell!" Wonder Woman tells the Master Mage.

The Amazon Princess drops the enormous loop down toward the City of the Golden Gate. The lasso settles around the entire the city.

"Now, Calculha!" Wonder Woman says.

The Master Mage grabs the end of the Lasso of Truth and sends magical energy along its length. The golden lasso blazes like a small sun. Calculha's spell reaches out from the lasso to enclose the city in a giant orb of protection.

"The city is safe from the earthquakes," Calculha says. "But they will continue to shake the area as long as the Zodiac network is out of balance."

"Then I'm going to have to stop the earthquakes," Wonder Woman says.

"How? Even my magic cannot do that!" Calculha says.

"I'm going to use something called science," Wonder Woman replies.

Turn the page.

From her position in the sky above the city, Wonder Woman can see the earthquake's seismic waves rolling across the surface of the landscape.

RUMBLE! RUMBLE! RUMBLE!

The tremors lift, and then lower, the trees of a nearby forest. The water of a large lake ripples and races from one shore to the other.

"This will be a test of how much I remember about wavelengths and amplitudes," Wonder Woman says.

Turn to page 62.

Wonder Woman surprises the hunters by grabbing onto Morgaine and launching into the air. She punches her way up through the trees and thick jungle growth until she reaches the open sky. Wonder Woman flies beyond the treetops before the startled men think to shoot.

"This is not a safe habitat," the Amazon warrior says.

Wonder Woman flies back to where they entered the habitat. It takes them a little while, but eventually they find the hatch hidden behind the vines and lush plant growth.

Wonder Woman and Morgaine enter the tunnel and walk until they come to the power core. Wonder Woman quickly steps through the hatch, but Morgaine hesitates before she enters the room.

"I don't know if it's safe for me to go in there," Morgaine says. "The Zodiac Crystals drained my magic the first time. Who knows what could happen next?"

Turn the page.

Suddenly they hear a buzzing sound. Several small robot drones fly toward Wonder Woman. Short metal tubes stick out all over their mechanical bodies. Wonder Woman stands still as one of the drones directs a beam of light at the Amazon Princess and scans her with it.

"These robots make me wonder if there's a crew or if this place is automated," Wonder Woman says to Morgaine. "We should look for a central control room."

ZZZT! ZZZT! ZZZT! The drones suddenly start shooting energy blasts at Wonder Woman from their many metal tubes. She deflects the blasts with her bracelets.

BDOW! BDOW! BDOW!

The drones zip through the air, trying to shoot at her from every angle. Wonder Woman moves with amazing speed as she dodges the energy blasts.

"Stay back, Morgaine. These must be defense drones. I must have triggered them when I came into the room," Wonder Woman says.

"I knew it wasn't safe to go in there," Morgaine says as she stays out of sight on the other side of the habitat hatch.

More robots swarm into the room to attack Wonder Woman.

"These drones are as pesky as mosquitoes," Wonder Woman says. "I'm just going to have to swat them."

The Amazon Princess takes her golden lasso and snaps it like a whip. The end of the lasso smacks one of the drones and knocks it into another drone.

SMAAAK! CRAACK! Both drones fall to the deck with a thud.

SMAAAK! CRAAAK! Wonder Woman snaps her lasso over and over again. It does not take long before all the drones lie motionless at her feet.

Turn to page 65.

Holding the Leo Crystal in one hand, Wonder Woman twirls her golden lasso in the other. Then she tosses it toward Morgaine and the Scorpion Crystal. The loop lands around the scorpion stone, and Wonder Woman snatches the second Zodiac Crystal out of Morgaine's reach.

"Nooo!" Morgaine shouts.

Wonder Woman snaps the lasso like a whip, and the Scorpion Crystal lands in her hand. Brought together again through time and space, the two crystals begin to blaze with light. A band of energy forms between them. Then a portal opens up.

"Uh-oh," Wonder Woman says.

SWOOSH!

The Zodiac Crystals pull Wonder Woman into the vortex. Morgaine le Fey leaps in after her.

Wonder Woman and Morgaine le Fey tumble out of the portal and into a large cave. The cavern walls glow with the soft light of thousands of raw crystals.

"Uhhh, where are we now?" Morgaine moans.

"I do not know, but we are not alone," Wonder Woman says.

An ancient woman with long gray hair stands in the center of the cave. She wears golden robes and holds a tall staff. Behind her, ten Zodiac Crystals float in midair.

"The rest of the Zodiac stones are here!" Morgaine says. "I will have power beyond imagination!"

"No. The Zodiac is under my protection," the old woman says. She gestures with the staff, and the crystals in Wonder Woman's hands fly out of her grasp.

"I will have the stones!" Morgaine declares and fires a bolt of magic at the ancient woman.

The old woman holds up her hand, and Morgaine's bolt fizzles.

FZZZZT!

"How . . . ?" Morgaine gasps.

Turn to page 61.

"She has the power of the full Zodiac," Wonder Woman realizes. "Be glad she chooses to use it wisely."

"The Zodiac is complete once more," the old woman says. "Thank you for returning the lost crystals. What do you wish as your reward?"

"Send us home," Wonder Woman says.

"No! I—," Morgaine starts to say, but the old woman waves her hand, and suddenly Wonder Woman and Morgaine are back in Egypt, where they started.

Wonder Woman quickly ties up Morgaine with the golden lasso.

"The lasso compels you to obey me," Wonder Woman says. "Now repair the damage you caused to the Great Sphinx."

Even Morgaine's magic cannot resist the power of the Lasso of Truth, and the sorceress begins to put the Sphinx back together.

THE END

To follow another path, turn to page 11.

Wonder Woman flies out across the landscape, following the waves rippling across the ground. Soon she is going as fast as they are.

"Good. I've calculated the speed of the waves," Wonder Woman says.

The Amazon Princess lands on a clear patch of ground and waits for a wave to pass. She is lifted, then lowered, as the wave crest travels under her feet. She waits for another wave crest to pass.

"Now I have the height of the wave and its length—its amplitude and wavelength," Wonder Woman says. "With this information, I can duplicate the wave."

Wonder Woman braces her feet firmly on the ground, getting ready for what she is about to do next.

"Seismic waves are like sound waves traveling through the ground. My bracelets can create sound waves too," Wonder Woman says. "All I have to do is create a counter wave that cancels out the seismic wave. No pressure."

Wonder Woman faces an oncoming seismic swell racing toward her. The ground lifts up like an ocean wave. Wonder Woman slams her Amazon bracelets together.

CLAAAAAANGGGG!

The sound is tremendous and is heard across the landscape. **CLAAAANGGGG!** Wonder Woman creates a second wave of sound.

CLAAANGG! CLAAANGG! Wonder Woman keeps making waves until she sees that the ground has stopped rolling.

"My ears are going to be ringing for a while," Wonder Woman says as she heads back toward the City of the Golden Gate.

When Wonder Woman returns to the city, she sees that Calculha has taken down the spell of protection. The landscape is cracked and broken, but it has stopped shaking. Calculha stands next to his weary dragon outside of the city, waiting for her. The Master Mage hands the Lasso of Truth to the Amazon Princess.

Turn the page.

"Your lasso is a marvel of magic unlike any I've seen in Atlantis," Calculha says. "But I would like to learn more about this skill called science."

"I will be glad to teach you," Wonder Woman says. "But first I have to find Morgaine le Fey and stop her evil plan."

"And I will be glad to help you," Calculha says. "But I have one question."

"Which is?" Wonder Woman says.

"Who *are* you?" Calculha asks.

"Me? I'm just a traveler from far, far away," Wonder Woman replies with a smile.

THE END

To follow another path, turn to page 11.

Wonder Woman stands alert and looks around for any more drones. She does not see any, but she spots a hatch labeled Bridge.

"The bridge is where I'll find the controls to this place," Wonder Woman says. "You can come out now, Morgaine. It's safe."

The sorceress comes out from behind the habitat hatch. **CLUNK!** She kicks one of the fallen drones as she walks over to Wonder Woman.

"I was not afraid, Amazon," Morgaine says. "If I still had my magic, these pests would be heaps of melted metal."

"I'm sure they would be. Now, let's go. I want to know just where the Leo Crystal has taken us and if we can even get back home," Wonder Woman says as she opens the bridge hatch.

Wonder Woman and Morgaine walk down another long tunnel. At the end of it they enter a room full of navigational controls and monitors. A window stretches across one whole wall. Beyond the window is the starry vacuum of outer space.

Turn the page.

"We're on a spaceship," Morgaine gasps in surprise.

"I had that figured out a while ago," Wonder Woman says.

"And you did not share that knowledge with me?" Morgaine complains.

Suddenly a short alien enters the room and confronts Wonder Woman and Morgaine. He points an energy blaster at them.

"Who are you and how did you get here?" he declares.

"Such a rude creature," Morgaine says and instinctively gestures for her magic.

The alien reacts to Morgaine's gesture and fires his weapon at her. *ZZZZAT!*

Wonder Woman leaps to block the blast with her bracelets. *BZIIING!*

The energy blast bounces back at the alien and strikes him. *POWW!* He is knocked out and falls to the deck.

"Why is everything on this ship trying to attack us?" Morgaine says.

Wonder Woman looks around the bridge.

"These monitors show the ship's cargo," Wonder Woman says. "According to Justice League reports I've seen, these are all stolen goods. We're on an interstellar pirate ship, which is probably stolen too."

"How do we get *off* this interstellar pirate ship?" Morgaine asks.

"Simple. We call the interstellar police," Wonder Woman says. She activates the ship's communications network and sends out a message. "Wonder Woman calling the Green Lantern Corps. Home in on this signal. We've captured a space pirate who needs to go to prison. Oh, and please tell the Green Lantern of Earth that we need a lift home."

THE END

To follow another path, turn to page 11.

Wonder Woman decides to head toward the white building. It has many levels and terraces, and she can see people living there. Wonder Woman flies high into the air so that she can watch them without being seen. At the same time, she looks for Morgaine.

"This place is amazing," Wonder Woman says. "I'm inside the pyramid, but it's a hundred times bigger than the outside. There's even a sky and clouds and everything. How is this possible?"

Wonder Woman watches the people go about their normal activities. She sees children playing. Everything seems peaceful.

"That's strange. I don't see Morgaine anywhere," Wonder Woman says. "And those people are acting like they haven't seen her, either. Maybe I made the wrong choice."

BLAAAM!

An explosion suddenly erupts near the top of the building. A figure surrounded by a big ball of magical energy rises out of the smoke.

"Oh, there she is," Wonder Woman says.

Morgaine le Fey holds the Leo Crystal in one hand. In her other hand she holds a crystal carved in the shape of a bull's head. The two gems blaze with light. Bolts of energy shoot out from the stones and into the sky.

ZABLAM! SHAZAK!

Suddenly the sky starts to tear apart like a ripped curtain. One of the rips opens up near Wonder Woman and nearly swallows her. She escapes, but not before she feels the bone-chilling cold of the nothingness within the rift.

"Whatever this place is, it's coming apart," Wonder Woman realizes.

Wonder Woman sees Morgaine hold the Zodiac Crystals above her head. Then she sends a blast down at the white building.

BLAAAAM!

The people on the terraces run for their lives. Wonder Woman speeds to their rescue.

Turn to page 71.

"Stop, Morgaine!" Wonder Woman says as she puts herself between the fleeing people and the sorceress. The Amazon Princess deflects Morgaine's blasts with her bracelets.

ZZZPOW! ZZZPOW!

The bolts shoot back toward Morgaine.

"I won't stop until I have all the crystals in the Zodiac!" Morgaine declares.

"I'll stop you," Wonder Woman says.

The Amazon Princess tosses her golden lasso toward the sorceress. Morgaine is surprised when the glowing rope pierces her orb of magical energy. The lasso loops around the bull's head crystal, and Wonder Woman yanks it out of Morgaine's grasp.

Turn to page 76.

The Zodiac Crystal of Mu floats in the air between Morgaine le Fey and Majistra. It is carved in the shape of twin pillars resting between two discs.

"The Gemini Crystal!" Majistra gasps. "So this is what you are after, strange sorcerer."

"Soon I will have all twelve Zodiac stones, and they will give me unlimited power," Morgaine says.

"Not if I can help it," Wonder Woman declares. She flies toward the floating Zodiac Crystal at tremendous speed. **ZOOOOM!**

The evil sorceress is startled to see the Amazon Princess.

"What? Wonder Woman!" Morgaine growls in surprise. "I thought I left you far behind me in the City of the Golden Gate."

"You should know by now that you can't escape me," Wonder Woman says.

The sorceress is filled with fury and fires a bolt of magical energy toward the hero.

Wonder Woman sees the danger heading her way. She uses one of her bracelets to deflect it back at Morgaine.

KZZAAAT! BLAAAM!

The sorceress is forced to defend herself against her own magic. Wonder Woman grabs the hovering Gemini Crystal. A few moments later she lands next to the Master Mage of Mu.

"Keep this safe while I deal with Morgaine," Wonder Woman says as she hands the Zodiac Crystal to Majistra.

Frustrated and angry, Morgaine transforms herself into a gigantic monster. It has enormous tentacles and several mouths full of sharp teeth. **ROAAAR!** It holds the Leo Crystal in one of its tentacles while it swipes at Wonder Woman and the Master Mage with the others.

Turn to page 79.

Wonder Woman decides that the armored figures are friendly. They came through the door marked Maintenance, and she guesses that they must be maintenance workers.

"We come in peace and need your help," Wonder Woman says.

"Who are you? Did you come from a habitat? Has there been a breach?" the first one asks.

"I will answer all of your questions," Wonder Woman replies. "But first, this woman needs medical attention."

"No I don't," Morgaine moans and struggles to escape Wonder Woman's embrace. "Put me down."

Wonder Woman sets the sorceress back on her feet.

"You have to get out of here. You can't be in the engine core unshielded," one of the armored figures says.

"I'm much tougher than I look," Wonder Woman says.

"Gwenda, I'm reading a power surge!" another of the armored figures says. "The core is out of balance."

"What caused that, Suzin?" Gwenda asks.

"I don't know, but we've got to realign the energy frequencies, or the core will explode," Suzin replies.

The armored figures suddenly forget about Wonder Woman and Morgaine and rush around the chamber. They feverishly work the controls on the machinery.

"The Zodiac Crystals in the energy core absorbed your magic, Morgaine," Wonder Woman says. "That's why the core is out of balance. The extra energy tipped the scales."

"Well, I want my magic back," Morgaine declares, marching toward the blazing core.

Turn to page 83.

Wonder Woman holds the bull's head crystal in her hands. Morgaine fires a giant bolt of magical energy at the Amazon, but the bull's head crystal soaks up the power.

SHOOM!

"This crystal just absorbed Morgaine's energy bolt. Let's see if I can use it against her," Wonder Woman says.

Wonder Woman flies toward Morgaine with the crystal in her fist. **POW!** She uses its powerful energies to punch through the sorceress's protective shield.

BAM! Wonder Woman's next blow strikes Morgaine. The sorceress is knocked out, and her energy shield dissolves. She lets go of the Leo Crystal, and it flies toward the bull's head stone in Wonder Woman's hand. The two crystals blaze with light, but the lightning bolts stop ripping up the sky.

Wonder Woman wraps up Morgaine in her golden lasso and lands on a terrace of the white building. A man approaches her nervously.

"Please! Return the Taurus Crystal to us or our world will collapse!" the man says.

"Taurus Crystal? Of course! Taurus is the Zodiac sign represented by the bull," Wonder Woman says as she hands over the bull's head crystal. The Leo Crystal tugs toward the Taurus stone, but Wonder Woman holds onto it.

"The Taurus Crystal is the power source that keeps our pocket dimension intact," the man explains. "I must return it to its energy cradle."

The man runs through the hole Morgaine blasted in the white building. A few minutes later the sky starts to repair itself. The man returns as people start to come out of the building.

"Thank you!" the man says. "I'm King Atlas, leader of New Atlantis. Who are you?"

"I am Princess Diana, daughter of Queen Hippolyta of Themyscira," Wonder Woman says. "I'd like to stay and learn more about this place, but I have to get back home and put this villain in jail. Her magic activated the Leo Crystal and sent us millions of years into Earth's past."

Turn the page.

"Oh, we can send you to any dimension, time, or reality," Atlas says. "We have the tech for that. Stay as long as you want. You can go home at any time."

"Then I'll stay for a bit," Wonder Woman says. "Besides, it looks like Morgaine is going to be asleep for a while."

THE END

To follow another path, turn to page 11.

"What a temper," Wonder Woman says as the Morgaine monster tries to smack her with a giant tentacle. Morgaine misses and smashes the side of a building instead. "Now see what you did? I'm going to have to put you in a time-out."

Wonder Woman grabs one of the tentacles. She uses her tremendous Amazon strength to flick it like a whip. The monster lifts into the air and then slams to the ground.

WHOOOMP!

The impact stuns Morgaine, but only for a few seconds. That is all the time Wonder Woman needs to use her amazing Amazon speed to snatch the Leo Crystal from the monster's grasp.

"Noooo!" Morgaine screams from her multiple monster mouths. She charges toward the Amazon Princess on all of her tentacles.

Wonder Woman tucks the Zodiac Crystal securely into her belt. Then she grabs her golden lasso and starts twirling it above her head.

Turn to page 81.

"I'm not afraid of your little lasso," Morgaine says with a sneer.

"It doesn't *stay* little," the Amazon warrior replies.

Wonder Woman leaps into the air and tosses the golden lasso toward the Morgaine monster. The loop expands and drops around the monster's massive body.

WHOOSH! WHOOSH! WHOOSH!

Wonder Woman zooms around and around the monster until it is wrapped up tightly.

"By the power of the Lasso of Truth, I compel you to surrender and return to your human form," Wonder Woman says.

The Morgaine monster shrinks as the sorceress returns to her normal size and form. The golden lasso shrinks with her.

"Your lasso has powerful magic," Majistra says as she comes to stand next to Wonder Woman.

Turn the page.

"I wish it had the power to send us back home," Wonder Woman says. "The Leo Crystal brought us here, but I don't know if it can get us back."

"It might be able to, if I combine it with the Gemini Crystal," Majistra says. "Give it to me."

Wonder Woman hands the Leo stone to the Master Mage. Majistra glows with brilliant magical energies.

"Such power! Now I know why the sorceress sought to possess the Zodiac!" Majistra says with a dark sounding laugh. "Now it is mine!"

"Oh no," Wonder Woman says. But before the hero can take back the stone, she and Morgaine are transported back to Egypt.

THE END

To follow another path, turn to page 11.

"Morgaine! No!" Wonder Woman shouts.

Wonder Woman runs after Morgaine. She uses her amazing speed to get in front of the sorceress and block her from reaching the core.

"Get out of my way you meddlesome Amazon," Morgaine snarls.

"The energies in the core will kill you," Wonder Woman says. "I'm just trying to save your life."

"Magic *is* my life!" Morgaine says.

The sorceress gestures toward the energy core and speaks an ancient spell of summoning. A ribbon of magical power comes out of the blazing sphere and twists through the air toward Morgaine.

WOOO! WOOO! WOOO! Alarms suddenly go off in the engine room.

"Now there's a power *drain!*" Gwenda shouts.

"I'm trying to adjust the energy levels in the core!" Suzin cries.

Turn the page.

"I'm losing containment!" Gwenda warns. "The core is going to explode!"

"If the energy core explodes, it might destroy the whole ship and all the habitats," Wonder Woman says. "I won't let you put these people in danger, Morgaine."

Wonder Woman turns to face the power core. She uses her silver Amazon bracelets to block the ribbon of magic from reaching Morgaine. Then she uses them like a shield to push the streamer back into the core.

"Nooo!" Morgaine screams.

The sorceress rushes toward Wonder Woman to attack her from behind, but the hero hears her coming. The Amazon spins and smacks Morgaine on her golden helmet. **CLAAANG!** Morgaine is stunned by the blow and falls to the deck.

"The core is still out of control. I've got to contain it before it explodes," Wonder Woman says. "And I know just how to do that."

Turn to page 86.

Wonder Woman flies around and around the core, wrapping it with her golden lasso. Soon it looks like a golden ball of string.

"Power levels are stabilizing!" Gwenda shouts.

"Containment field is intact," Suzin says. "The core is back in balance."

"Thank you, stranger," Gwenda says as she comes over to Wonder Woman and stares at the lasso-wrapped energy core.

"Well, we sort of created the problem in the first place, so it's only right that I solve it," Wonder Woman says. "Now if only I could solve the problem of how to get back to Earth."

"Earth? That's the planet our colony ship is going to invade," Gwenda says. "Who *are* y—?"

POWWW!

Wonder Woman slams the armored enemy and begins her new battle to save Earth.

THE END

To follow another path, turn to page 11.

"That black building looks like a giant vault, which is where I would keep a powerful Zodiac Crystal for safekeeping," Wonder Woman says.

Suddenly a huge fireball strikes the black structure from the air. **BOOM!**

Wonder Woman sees Morgaine above the building, bombarding it with magical energy.

BLAAAM! BLAAAM!

"It looks like Morgaine thinks the same thing," Wonder Woman says.

The Amazon Princess flies toward the building, but before she can get there Morgaine blasts an opening in the building and disappears inside. Wonder Woman doubles her speed and zooms though the opening only a few seconds after Morgaine. The sorceress stands in front of a pedestal. On it rests a crystal carved in the shape of a ram's head.

"The Aries Crystal! Together with the Leo stone, my magical power will be doubled!" Morgaine says.

Turn the page.

"Not if I can help it," Wonder Woman declares.

Wonder Woman leaps toward the Aries Crystal as Morgaine reaches for it. Using her Amazon speed, Wonder Woman grabs the gem before Morgaine.

"Stop interfering, Amazon!" Morgaine growls.

The furious sorceress uses the Leo Crystal to fire a giant blast of magic at Wonder Woman. The Amazon Princess raises her bracelets to deflect the bolt, but it never reaches her. Instead, the ram's head crystal sucks up the magical energy. Then the stone bursts with brilliant light. When it fades, there is something else in the chamber with them.

Turn to page 96.

Wonder Woman zips toward Morgaine le Fey. The Amazon Princess becomes a blur of motion that the sorceress does not see coming. Wonder Woman rams into Morgaine.

BWHAAAAM!

Morgaine is knocked far across the sky. The impact is so great that the Leo Crystal flies out of her hand.

"Got you," Wonder Woman says as she catches the gem.

Wonder Woman lands next to Majistra and hands her the Leo Crystal.

"Keep the Zodiac Crystals safe while I take care of Morgaine," Wonder Woman says.

"Who are you? Where did you come from?" Majistra asks.

"I'll fill you in later," Wonder Woman says. "This fight isn't over yet."

Suddenly Morgaine le Fey appears in a blaze of magic.

Turn the page.

"You caught me by surprise, Wonder Woman. It will not happen again," Morgaine says.

"We'll see about that," Wonder Woman replies.

The Amazon Princess launches toward Morgaine. The sorceress surrounds herself with a glowing globe of magical protection. Wonder Woman hits it with all of her strength.

POWWW!

The force of her blow makes the orb crackle and spark, but it does not break.

"Ha! You cannot break through my spell," Morgaine taunts.

"Maybe not, but I have more than one trick up my sleeve," Wonder Woman says.

The Amazon Princess claps her bracelets together. **CLAAANG!**

A wave of sonic force hits Morgaine's orb of protection. The orb and Morgaine are knocked high into the sky like a baseball hit by a bat.

"If I can keep Morgaine away from the city and busy fighting me, she won't go after the Zodiac Crystals," Wonder Woman says as she flies after the sorceress.

Wonder Woman catches up to the hurtling orb in midair. She twirls her golden lasso and snags the globe of magical energy.

"Let's go for a spin," Wonder Woman says as she whirls the lasso in circles above her head.

Inside the orb, Morgaine starts to get dizzy.

"Enough!" Morgaine shouts.

The sorceress ends her protection spell with an explosion.

BWAAAM!

The force of the blast tumbles Wonder Woman, but she recovers quickly and flies toward Morgaine at tremendous speed.

Turn to page 99.

Wonder Woman looks at the armored suits and blaster-like objects they hold. She worries that these people might not be friendly, and that she will have to fight them to protect Morgaine. She knows there is one way to find out.

Wonder Woman throws her golden Lasso of Truth around the armored figures. The glowing rope binds them.

"The lasso compels you to speak the truth," Wonder Woman says. "Are you my foes?"

"No," one of the figures replies.

"Why are you wearing armor?" Wonder Woman asks.

"These are radiation suits," another figure says. "We are engineers and need them to maintain the energy core."

Wonder Woman looks at the blazing orb that surrounds the three Zodiac Crystals.

"Radiation? That's all the more reason to get Morgaine out of here," Wonder Woman says.

Wonder Woman releases the armored figures and carries Morgaine through the maintenance hatch. She runs down a long tunnel until she reaches another hatch. This one is unlocked. Wonder Woman opens it and enters a room filled with tools and maintenance equipment.

Morgaine starts to wake up, and Wonder Woman sets her back on her feet. **BWAAM!** Suddenly the floor shudders. **BWAAM!** A second shock rocks them. The armored maintenance staff runs out of the tunnel.

"What happened?" Wonder Woman asks.

"The Krayzon are attacking us again!" one of the engineers says.

"Maybe I can help," Wonder Woman says.

"You? How?" the engineer asks doubtfully.

"I have . . . abilities," Wonder Woman says.

"She has fought gods and won," Morgaine admits.

"I'll take you to the command module," the engineer decides.

Turn the page.

A few minutes later, they stand in the command module, and the situation becomes clear. Wonder Woman looks out a view port at habitat domes arranged in a vast ring around a central engine core.

"This is a space ark," Wonder Woman says.

Small attack ships swarm around the ark, shooting energy blasts at the vessel.

"I can stop those ships," Wonder Woman says. "But I have to get outside."

"Use the emergency airlock," the engineer says, pointing to a nearby hatch.

Wonder Woman enters the airlock and, moments later, launches from its exterior hatch toward the enemy ships. She flies like a missile and punches one of the fighters.

KBAAAM!

The fighter ship tumbles end over end and slams into another fighter.

CRAAASH!

Turn to page 103.

A huge creature looms over Wonder Woman and Morgaine. It has a humanlike body but the head and hooves of a ram. It stretches out its arms and tilts back its head.

"I am free! Freeee!" the creature shouts.

"What strange monster is this?" Morgaine le Fey asks.

"I don't know, but it can't be good," Wonder Woman replies.

"I have been enslaved within the crystal since the days of Atlantis," the creature says. "You have released me, and as thanks I will make your deaths painless."

"No one is dying today, monster," Wonder Woman says. "Morgaine, if we work together, we can put this genie back in its bottle. Morgaine?"

But the sorceress is gone, and so is the Aries Crystal.

"I will not go back into the Darkness!" the Aries monster says.

The creature rushes at Wonder Woman. **WHAAAM!** It butts the Amazon with its powerful horns. Wonder Woman crashes against the wall of the chamber.

"Uhhh. You are strong," Wonder Woman says as she gets to her feet. "But it will take more than that to hurt me."

The monster rushes at Wonder Woman again, but this time she leaps out of the way.

BOOM! The Aries demon smashes into the wall with such force that the building starts to collapse! Wonder Woman flies out of the hole blasted by Morgaine and escapes. The Aries monster does not.

"Not the Darknessss!" the monster howls as it becomes trapped within the building's rubble.

"Now where did Morgaine go?" Wonder Woman says.

The sorceress is not far away. Wonder Woman finds her struggling to use the Aries Crystal to open a portal to the next Zodiac gem.

Turn the page.

"This stone is useless! It has no magical power without the demon inside of it," Morgaine says in frustration.

Morgaine is so distracted by the crystal's failure that she doesn't realize that Wonder Woman has snared her with the golden lasso.

"The Lasso of Truth compels you to obey me," Wonder Woman says.

Morgaine struggles against the rope, but its power is stronger than her magic.

"Now you will use your sorcery to return us to where—and when—we came from. Back to Egypt!" Wonder Woman says.

"I will obey," Morgaine says and blazes with magical energy.

THE END

To follow another path, turn to page 11.

Morgaine le Fey fires bolts of magic at the Amazon Princess as fast as she can, but Wonder Woman dodges them just as fast. Seconds later she punches Morgaine on her golden mask.

BWAAANG!

Morgaine hurtles toward the ground. Suddenly the ground transforms into two giant hands that safely catch Morgaine. Wonder Woman swoops down and smashes them out from under the sorceress.

"You will not defeat me, Wonder Woman," Morgaine says as she lowers herself gently to the ground.

"Then *we* will," a voice says from above.

Morgaine looks up to see Majistra standing on a disc of magical energy. Eleven other men and women float beside her on similar glowing platforms.

"And who are you?" Morgaine sneers.

"We are the Master Mages of the Twelve Cities of Atlantis," one of the men says.

Turn the page.

"Calculha!" Wonder Woman says, recognizing the man. "Welcome to the party."

"You endanger the Zodiac and must be stopped," Majistra says.

"Nothing can stop me," Morgaine says as she unleashes a gigantic bolt of magical energy at the mages hovering above her.

Wonder Woman moves with her amazing Amazon speed to put herself between the bolt and the mages. She crosses her bracelets in front of her. She uses them like a shield to block the powerful blast and protect Calculha and the others.

SSSZZZZ!

Then Wonder Woman slowly forces her way down toward Morgaine until the sorceress faces her own blazing fire.

With a powerful push of her bracelets, Wonder Woman shoves Morgaine's blast back at the sorceress.

BLAAAM!

Turn to page 102.

Morgaine is hit with her own magical bolt. She is knocked out and falls to the ground. Wonder Woman lands and stands over her defeated foe. The twelve mages float down from above and surround the fallen sorceress.

"The Zodiac Crystals are safe," Calculha says.

"And this sorceress will be punished for her deeds," Majistra says.

"Yes, she most definitely will—if I can get us both back to where and when we came from," Wonder Woman says.

"That task should not be difficult for the combined powers of twelve Master Mages," Calculha says.

FWOOOSH!

A moment later, Wonder Woman stands in front of the Great Sphinx with Morgaine le Fey at her feet.

"No, not difficult at all," Wonder Woman says.

THE END

To follow another path, turn to page 11.

Wonder Woman twirls her golden lasso as two more fighters zoom past her, firing their energy weapons at the space ark. ***ZZAAT! ZZAAT!***

The Amazon Princess snags the fighters with her lasso and spins them above her head. Then she releases them, and the ships crash into more fighters. ***SMAAASH!***

Wonder Woman flies at tremendous speed toward a group of attacking ships. They finally realize that she is a threat and fire their weapons at her.

ZZAAT! ZZAAT!

Wonder Woman uses her bracelets to deflect the energy blasts back at the ships.

KBOOOM! Their engines explode, and the ships drift harmlessly in space.

The rest of the fighter ships give up the battle and flee. Wonder Woman sees that they are heading for a large mothership.

I can't let them leave this mess, Wonder Woman thinks.

Turn the page.

She scoops up all the damaged and drifting enemy fighters with her lasso and heads toward the giant vessel. Wonder Woman tosses all the small fighter ships into the larger vessel's landing bay. Then she grabs the hull with both hands.

CRUNCH! CRUNCH! Her fingers dig into the metal.

Wonder Woman uses her tremendous Amazon strength to swing the alien mothership like a giant Olympic discus and throw it far away from the space ark. It disappears out of sight into the darkness of deep space.

Wonder Woman returns to the space ark. Morgaine and the command crew are waiting for her when she steps out of the airlock.

"Thank you!" the captain says. "You have saved thousands of lives. How can we possibly repay you?"

"You could help us get back home to Earth," Wonder Woman says.

"Earth?! Our ancestors were from Earth!" the captain says. "They left the planet thousands of years ago."

"These people are using Atlantean Zodiac Crystals, which makes me think that their ancestors were probably from Atlantis," Morgaine says.

"Yes, they were," the captain says. "And we have never lost contact with the Royal City."

"I happen to know the current King of Atlantis," Wonder Woman says. "His name is Aquaman, and I'd like to send him a message."

"Of course. What is your message?" the captain asks.

"Please tell him to send the Justice League spaceship," Wonder Woman says. "It's time to go home."

THE END

To follow another path, turn to page 11.

AUTHOR

Laurie S. Sutton has been reading comics since she was a kid. She grew up to become an editor for Marvel, DC Comics, Starblaze, and Tekno Comics. She has written *Adam Strange* for DC, *Star Trek: Voyager* for Marvel, plus *Star Trek: Deep Space Nine* and *Witch Hunter* for Malibu Comics. There are long boxes of comics in her closet where there should be clothing and shoes. Laurie has lived all over the world, and currently resides in Florida.

ILLUSTRATOR

Omar Lozano lives in Monterrey, Mexico. He has always been crazy for illustration and is constantly on the lookout for awesome things to draw. In his free time, he watches lots of movies, reads fantasy and sci-fi books, and draws! Omar has worked for Marvel, DC, IDW, Capstone, and several other publishing companies.

GLOSSARY

amplitude (AM-pluh-tood)—the distance from the midpoint of a wave to its crest

amulet (AM-yoo-let)—a small charm believed to protect the wearer from harm

ancestors (AN-ses-ters)—ones from whom an individual, group, or species is descended

automated (AW-tuh-may-ted)—operated by machines rather than people

habitat (HAB-uh-tat)—the home of a plant or animal

humanoid (HYOO-muh-noid)—shaped somewhat like a human

intercept (in-tur-SEPT)—to stop the movement of an object

interstellar (in-tur-STEL-uhr)—happening or located between stars

mage (MAYJ)—a magician

portal (POHR-tuhl)—a large, impressive opening or entrance

prehistoric (pree-hi-STOR-ik)—from a time before history was recorded

radiation (ray-dee-AY-shuhn)—rays of energy given off by certain elements

vacuum (VAK-yoom)—space that is completely empty of all matter, including air and other gases

vortex (VOHR-tex)—air or light moving in a circular motion

MORGAINE LE FEY

Birthplace:
England

Occupation:
Sorceress

Species:
Human

Height:
5 feet 10 inches

Weight:
156 pounds

Eyes:
Black

Hair:
Black

Powers/Abilities:
A deadly sorceress, able to teleport, read minds,
shoot energy bolts from her fingertips, and
harness magic.

As the half-sister of the medieval ruler King Arthur, Morgaine le Fey has lived for hundreds of years. The evil sorceress maintains her immortality with powerful black magic, but her beauty could not be saved. To hide her old, withering body, Morgaine wears a suit of golden armor. However, she is not satisfied and will stop at nothing to regain her looks.

- As Morgaine continues to age, the body beneath her golden armor weakens. To survive, and one day regain her youthful appearance, the evil sorceress must drain life from others. Over the centuries, she's been known to steal youthful energy from both humans and super heroes.

- Morgaine once attempted to rob Wonder Woman of her life force. She believed the Amazon Princess possessed immortal energy. However, Wonder Woman had given up her immortality upon leaving the island of Themyscira. When the sorceress attacked the super hero, Morgaine's evil plan backfired, and she turned to dust. Unfortunately, she soon returned, seeking revenge.

- Using black magic, also known as dark arts, Morgaine has mastered several remarkable powers of the mind. Telepathy lets her communicate using her mind alone. Telekenesis allows her to move objects from one place to another with only her mind. Teleportation gives Morgaine the power to use her mind to transport people and objects to other places and times.

←YOU CHOOSE→

WONDER WOMAN

Morgaine le Fey has found a magical Zodiac Crystal. But when Wonder Woman battles the sorceress for control of it, the duo gets sucked into an energy portal. Now it's up to you to help the Amazon warrior foil Morgaine le Fey's schemes during *The Crystal Quest!*

Follow the directions at the bottom of each page. The choices YOU make will change the outcome of the story. After you finish one path, go back and read the others for more Wonder Woman adventures!

Wonder Woman sits with her mother, Queen Hippolyta, on a balcony of the royal palace atop the highest hill in Themyscira. They are enjoying dinner together as they watch a beautiful sunset.

"I am glad to have this time with you, daughter. I don't get to see you very much now that you have gone to the outside world," Hippolyta says.

"My duties with the Justice League keep me very busy," Wonder Woman says. "They have sworn to battle evil, and I stand with them in their fight."

"They have the finest Amazon warrior among them," Hippolyta says.

"Oh, Mother, you are exaggerating," Wonder Woman says and smiles.

BZZZT! The Justice League communicator on Wonder Woman's belt signals for her attention.

"Wonder Woman, it's Batman calling from the Watchtower," a man's voice says.

Turn the page.

Wonder Woman glances up at the sky. The Watchtower is the Justice League's headquarters in orbit above Earth.

"Is there an emergency, Batman?" Wonder Woman asks.

"Yes. The Great Sphinx in Egypt is under attack, and people are in danger. You're needed," the Dark Knight says.

"I am on my way," Wonder Woman replies. She turns to Hippolyta. "I must go, Mother."

"Go swiftly and fight well," says Hippolyta.

Wonder Woman leaps from the palace balcony and streaks into the sky. She flies at super-speed and arrives at the Great Sphinx in no time. The magnificent monument is being torn apart!

BLAAAM! BLAAM!

A woman dressed in a purple gown and a golden helmet casts bolts of bright energy that blast the ancient statue. Wonder Woman recognizes the super-villain.

"It's the evil sorceress, Morgaine le Fey!" Wonder Woman says. "She's been around since the days of King Arthur and has many magical abilities. And she's using them to destroy the Great Sphinx!"

Wonder Woman flies between Morgaine and the Sphinx. She uses her Amazon bracelets to deflect the energy bolts back at the villain.

ZZPOW! ZZBAM!

Morgaine is forced to dodge her own destructive bolts.

"I don't know what you're up to, but I'm here to stop you," Wonder Woman says.

The Amazon Princess flies at Morgaine at amazing speed.

ZWOOOOSH!

At the same time, Wonder Woman claps her silver bracelets together. They make a sonic wave of sound. **CLAAANG!** The sorceress is knocked out of the sky. She lands with a thump on the desert sands.

Turn the page.

"Give up?" Wonder Woman asks as she hovers above the super-villain.

"No," Morgaine says. She gets to her feet and fires a final bolt. The blast blows the head of the Sphinx apart, revealing a glowing artifact floating in midair. It is a large crystal disc carved in the shape of a lion's head.

"That's what you're after? It doesn't look like much," Wonder Woman says.

"It's an Atlantean Zodiac Crystal," Morgaine says. "It's one of twelve hidden stones that will boost my magical power to incredible levels."

Morgaine flies toward the floating gem. Wonder Woman zooms to intercept her. They both grab the stone at the same time.

"Hands off, Wonder Woman!" Morgaine says. "This Leo Crystal will take me to other Zodiac stones. And once they are all brought together, my magic will be unlimited!"

The sorceress starts to glow with powerful energies.

"I won't let that happen," Wonder Woman replies. She uses her Amazon strength to pull the gem from Morgaine's grasp.

The Leo Crystal suddenly blazes like a small sun in Wonder Woman's hands. Then a swirling vortex forms around the Amazon Princess.

"My magic activated the crystal!" Morgaine realizes. "It's opening a portal leading to the next Zodiac gem!"

The sorceress makes a final grab for the crystal. She and Wonder Woman hold onto the gem as it flies into the portal—and takes both of them with it. But to *where?*

If Wonder Woman and Morgaine end up in the Jurassic period, turn to page 12.

If Wonder Woman and Morgaine arrive in ancient Atlantis, turn to page 14.

If Wonder Woman and Morgaine find themselves on a space ark, turn to page 16.

Wonder Woman and Morgaine le Fey tumble through a black void. They have no idea where they are. All they know is that the Leo Crystal is taking them to another Zodiac stone.

Suddenly they drop out of the void and land on solid ground. **THWUUUMP!** They are surprised to see a herd of triceratops surrounding them!

"We've traveled through time!" Wonder Woman says. "By the looks of these dinosaurs, we're in the Jurassic period!"

"I don't care where or when we are. I want that crystal!" Morgaine says, lunging for the gem.

Wonder Woman launches into the sky to keep the stone away from the sorceress. Morgaine flies after her. Wonder Woman is startled to feel the gem drag her through the air. Then she sees that it is taking her toward a pyramid.

What's a pyramid doing in the Jurassic period? Wonder Woman thinks. *I bet someone used a Zodiac Crystal to build it. That must be where another Zodiac gem is hidden. I can't let the two stones meet.*

Wonder Woman uses her Amazon strength to carry the Zodiac Crystal away from the pyramid. The stone tugs against her grip. Morgaine follows Wonder Woman, not seeing the pyramid or realizing that it might contain a second gem.

Morgaine fires bolts of magical energy at the Amazon Princess.

ZZAPOW! ZZAPOW!

Wonder Woman grips the Zodiac stone with both hands and holds up her bracelets to deflect the blasts as best she can.

"The power of the Zodiac will be mine!" Morgaine declares and fires a tremendous bolt of magic at Wonder Woman.

The bolt is too large for Wonder Woman to deflect or dodge. It hits her with enormous force.

"Uhhh!" Wonder Woman moans. Her grip loosens around the crystal.

If Wonder Woman holds onto the crystal, turn to page 18.
If Wonder Woman lets go of the crystal, turn to page 25.

When the portal opens again Wonder Woman and Morgaine le Fey are in the middle of a wide avenue crowded with people. Wonder Woman has no time to look at her surroundings before Morgaine attacks her.

BWAAAM! Morgaine fires a bolt of magical energy at the Amazon Princess. Wonder Woman deflects the bolt with one of her bracelets. The blast explodes harmlessly in the air above the crowd, but the people react with shock and fear.

"Give me that crystal, Wonder Woman!" Morgaine demands.

The sorceress does not wait for Wonder Woman to reply. She shoots another powerful bolt at the Amazon.

"Halt!" a man's voice commands.

A man riding a tame dragon lands near Wonder Woman and Morgaine.

"I am Calculha, Master Mage and Protector of the City of the Golden Gate," he says. "Stop your battle!"

"The City of the Golden Gate? I know that name from Amazon legend," Wonder Woman says. "I'm in one of the major cities on the ancient continent of Atlantis!"

Suddenly Calculha sees the crystal in Wonder Woman's hand.

"How did you get the Leo Crystal? It must not be removed from under the city!" Calculha says in shock. "It will bring destruction to the entire Zodiac network of magic!"

"Of course! Because we've traveled to the past, the original Leo Crystal is still *here!*" Morgaine realizes. She uses her magic to crack open the ground and call the original Leo Crystal to her hand.

An earthquake immediately shakes the whole city. Buildings start to collapse around people. As Morgaine flies away with the Atlantean crystal, Wonder Woman must choose between staying to rescue people or going after Morgaine.

If Wonder Woman stays to rescue people, turn to page 20.
If Wonder Woman goes after Morgaine, turn to page 27.

As soon as the portal closes behind Wonder Woman and Morgaine, another one opens. The Leo Crystal pulls them through it and onto a metal deck. Above their heads, a gigantic ball of blazing energy slowly rotates inside an enormous metal web. Wonder Woman and Morgaine both feel its intense heat and light. Inside the brilliant orb are three even brighter spots of light.

"The Leo stone has found not just one Zodiac Crystal but three!" Morgaine says.

"It looks like they're creating an energy field," Wonder Woman says. Then she sees that they are in a room full of machinery. "I think we're in a power core of some kind."

"That power will be mine!" Morgaine declares and tries to fire a bolt of magical energy at the orb. But nothing comes out of her hands.

"What? What happened to my magic?" Morgaine gasps in surprise.

"What's happening to the Leo Crystal?" Wonder Woman asks. The Zodiac stone glows a fiery red in her hands.

Wonder Woman tosses the crystal across the room just before it explodes.

BOOM!

"The Leo Crystal overloaded," Wonder Woman says. "It couldn't handle the energy of the other three crystals."

"The crystals . . . they're draining the magic out of me," Morgaine says as she collapses.

"I've got to get you out of here," Wonder Woman says. She lifts the limp sorceress into her arms and looks for a way out of the room. She sees several hatches labeled Habitat One, Habitat Two, Habitat Three, and so on.

"I think we're on a spaceship," Wonder Woman says as she decides which door to choose.

If Wonder Woman opens the door to Habitat One, turn to page 23.

If Wonder Woman selects the door to Habitat Two, turn to page 29.

Wonder Woman feels her fingers losing their grasp on the Zodiac Crystal. She doubles her effort to hold onto the gem. Morgaine's powerful magical energy ripples over the Amazon's body and is absorbed by the gem.

"Surrender the stone!" Morgaine demands.

"Never," Wonder Woman replies.

SCREEEEECH! Suddenly a giant pterodactyl flaps through the air toward Wonder Woman and Morgaine le Fey. Their battle has taken them too close to its nest. The creature snaps its long beak in warning.

"What monster is this?" Morgaine asks in surprise as the pterodactyl swoops toward her. She halts her attack on Wonder Woman for a moment.

The Amazon Princess takes advantage of Morgaine's brief distraction and zooms away from the sorceress. Realizing her mistake, Morgaine changes herself into a winged Hydra and flies after her foe.

As Wonder Woman speeds away, she sees a whole flock of pterodactyls. They now circle over their large nesting site. Below them, Wonder Woman spots hundreds of eggs half-buried in the sandy soil. The hero does not want to endanger them in her battle with Morgaine, so she starts to turn aside.

FWOOOOSH! Suddenly a stream of blazing fire shoots past her.

"Surrender the stone, or I will roast those creatures and their nests," Morgaine says.

Wonder Woman turns and sees the sorceress in Hydra form hovering near the nesting site. The villain shoots a blast of fire breath in warning. The pterodactyls fly in confusion and fear above their nests.

I can't let Morgaine harm those creatures, Wonder Woman thinks. *But should I let her have the crystal to save them? What do I do?*

If Wonder Woman defends the pterodactyl nests, turn to page 32.
If Wonder Woman surrenders the crystal, turn to page 49.

Wonder Woman decides that she can't leave while there are people in danger. She sees a building start to fall toward a crowd. The people try to run away, but the structure is too big for them to escape.

"Don't worry, everyone! I'm here to help you!" Wonder Woman says.

The Amazon Princess flies toward them at amazing speed and uses her Amazon strength to hold up the building. Her action gives the people just enough time to flee.

"Your strength is mighty," Calculha says as he soars on his dragon. "But so is my magic."

A glowing globe of magical energy extends out from the Master Mage to surround the structure that Wonder Woman holds. She is surprised when the building lifts out of her grasp and floats in midair. Then it turns to dust.

A moment later, the hero sees a giant crack in the ground heading toward another group of people. She tosses her golden lasso toward them. It expands to encircle the whole group.

Turn to page 22.

Wonder Woman tugs on the lasso and pulls everyone to safety. But as she hovers in the air, she sees that there are thousands more who need help.

"Calculha! The earthquake is destroying the city," Wonder Woman says. "If we want to save everyone, we have to stop the earthquake. Do you have a spell for that?"

"No. But you could use either the Leo Crystal or that amazing rope to save the city," Calculha replies.

"I am going to need your help," Wonder Woman says.

If Wonder Woman uses the Leo Crystal, turn to page 34.
If Wonder Woman uses her golden lasso, turn to page 52.

Wonder Woman turns the latch on the door labeled Habitat One. She steps into a long tunnel. The hero can see a small spot of light in the distance, and she walks toward it. When she reaches it, she sees the light is shining on another hatch door.

"This must be Habitat One," Wonder Woman says as she opens the hatch.

On the other side, the doorway is covered in a tangle of vines. Wonder Woman pushes through them carrying Morgaine.

"Well, it looks like Habitat One is a jungle," Wonder Woman says as she finds herself surrounded by lush plant life.

Morgaine slowly wakes up. As the sorceress wobbles on weak legs, Wonder Woman sees a dot of light travel across the villain's gold helmet.

"That's a targeting laser! Look out!" Wonder Woman warns.

ZZAPOW! A blast from an energy weapon speeds toward Morgaine.

Turn the page.

Wonder Woman leaps in front of the sorceress. **BZIIING!** She deflects the bolt with her bracelets and aims the blast back to its source.

"Arrrgh!" a voice shouts.

When Wonder Woman and Morgaine investigate, they find a stunned man on the ground. He is dressed in strange armor with an energy rifle nearby. Moments later they are surrounded by more men in armor. They aim their energy weapons at Wonder Woman and Morgaine.

"You are strange prey," the leader says.

"What do you mean . . . *prey?*" Morgaine demands.

"You are in the Hunting Ground. If you are not hunters you are prey," the leader says. "You have two choices: be hunted or die."

"I don't like those choices," Wonder Woman says. "I have a better idea."

If Wonder Woman and Morgaine fight the hunters, turn to page 36.

If Wonder Woman and Morgaine escape the hunters, turn to page 55.

Morgaine fires another big blast of magical energy at Wonder Woman. ***BZZOOW!*** The Zodiac Crystal soaks up the power and leaps from her hands. The Amazon Princess is forced to let go of the crystal. The stone zooms through the air, away from Morgaine and Wonder Woman. They both fly after it.

"The gem is heading for that pyramid," Morgaine realizes as the crystal speeds toward a structure in the distance. "It looks like one of the pyramids near the Great Sphinx in Egypt. Another Zodiac stone must be inside!"

Wonder Woman thinks the same thing.

"I can't let her reach that pyramid," Wonder Woman says.

The Amazon tosses her golden lasso and catches Morgaine around her legs. Before the sorceress can react, Wonder Woman twirls Morgaine around and around above her head.

"Oooh . . . ," Morgaine moans, getting dizzy. Then she gets mad.

Turn the page.

A giant eruption of magical energy explodes out from Morgaine. **KLABAAAAM!** The blast slams Wonder Woman to the ground. The golden lasso falls beside her. When Wonder Woman recovers, Morgaine le Fey is gone.

"She must be at the pyramid," Wonder Woman says and leaps into the air. When she arrives at the pyramid, she sees a huge hole blasted open in its side. "Yes, Morgaine is definitely here."

Wonder Woman steps into the pyramid. She is amazed at what she sees. The pyramid is bigger on the inside than on the outside! She sees a white building and a black building in the distance.

"The next Zodiac Crystal could be in one of those buildings," Wonder Woman says. "But which one?"

If Wonder Woman goes to the white building, turn to page 68.
If Wonder Woman goes to the black building, turn to page 87.

Wonder Woman is torn. She won't leave when there are people in danger. But she does not want to let Morgaine escape with the Atlantean Zodiac Crystal.

"Give me your Leo Crystal so I can save the city!" Calculha says.

Wonder Woman decides that the Master Mage knows how to use the Zodiac stone better than she does, so she hands over the gem. Calculha immediately glows with magical power. The energy spreads out all over the City of the Golden Gate. In a few moments the earthquakes stop.

"It looks like you know what you're doing," Wonder Woman tells Calculha. "I feel all right about leaving to go after Morgaine. If she removes another Zodiac Crystal, the whole continent of Atlantis could be destroyed. But I have no idea where she went."

"I can use the Leo Crystal to locate her and send you there," Calculha says. Images form in the air above the stone. "She is in Mu, battling Majistra, the Master Mage of that city."

Turn the page.

"Please, send me there," Wonder Woman says.

FWOOOSH! An instant later, Wonder Woman is in the city of Mu. She sees Morgaine and Majistra battling each other with bolts of searing magical energy.

"It looks like Morgaine has met her match," Wonder Woman says. "Still, I think the Master Mage of Mu would be glad to have my help to defeat Morgaine."

But before Wonder Woman can help Majistra, the ground cracks open and Mu's Zodiac Crystal rises into the air.

"Oh no! She's doing it again!" Wonder Woman says. "I have to do something, but what?"

If Wonder Woman tries to get to Mu's Zodiac Crystal first, turn to page 72.

If Wonder Woman tries to keep Morgaine away from Mu's Zodiac Crystal, turn to page 89.

Wonder Woman decides to try the hatch nearest to her, the one labeled Habitat Two. She holds Morgaine with one arm and grasps the latch with her free hand. But the latch won't move. Wonder Woman cannot open the door.

"It's locked," Wonder Woman realizes. She sees a keypad on the wall nearby. "There must be a code to open the door. A code I don't have."

Wonder Woman quickly looks at the other hatches. They all have keypads.

"There's got to be a way out of here," Wonder Woman says. "I just have to find it."

Wonder Woman works her way around the room. She tries the latch on each door, but none will open. Then she arrives at a hatch that is not like the others.

"Maintenance," Wonder Woman says as she reads the label on the extra-large door. She reaches for the latch.

CLICK! The door suddenly opens. But Wonder Woman has not touched the latch.

Turn the page.

Several large humanoids dressed in robot armor charge through the doorway. Wonder Woman jumps out of the way to avoid being knocked down. Her action catches the attention of the humanoids in armor.

"Who are you? How did you get in here? This is a radioactive area!" one of them says.

"There was an explosion. Did you cause it?" another one asks.

They point what look like energy blasters at Wonder Woman and Morgaine. Wonder Woman must decide if these humanoids are friends or foes.

If Wonder Woman decides they are friendly, turn to page 74.
If Wonder Woman thinks they are foes, turn to page 92.

"I must protect those innocent pterodactyls from Morgaine," Wonder Woman decides. "But I need to keep a hold of the Zodiac Crystal at the same time."

Wonder Woman slips the gem into her belt and tightly wraps her golden lasso around her waist to keep the stone in place. Now her hands are free, and Wonder Woman can use her bracelets to her full advantage.

The Amazon Princess claps the bracelets together. **BAWOOOOM!** A powerful sonic wave rushes toward the Morgaine dragon. **THWOMP!** The sonic force hits Morgaine, and she tumbles through the air. **THUUUD!** She hits the ground in a tangle of wings, claws, and tail.

"Roaaar!" the Morgaine Hydra bellows in frustration. Then her body shifts into another shape.

Morgaine changes from a Hydra into a giant hippogriff. She has the head, wings, and talons of an eagle in the front and the body of a horse in the back.

In her new form, the villain launches into the air to attack Wonder Woman. Morgaine claws at the hero with sharp talons and snaps her beak.

Good! As long as Morgaine is fighting me, she's not harming the pterodactyls, Wonder Woman thinks as she dodges Morgaine's monster form. *Now to lead her away from the nests.*

Wonder Woman speeds away. To make sure that Morgaine follows her, Wonder Woman flies backward and waves at the transformed sorceress.

"How dare you taunt me!" Morgaine shrieks and flaps after the Amazon Princess.

Turn to page 38.

"The Leo Crystal must be returned to its spot beneath the City of the Golden Gate," Calculha says. "That will restore the balance of the Zodiac network."

"That sounds like a good plan," Wonder Woman decides. She holds up the Leo stone. "Show me how to get there."

"I will take you there, but we must hurry. There is not much time left before the City of the Golden Gate is destroyed," Calculha says.

The Master Mage surrounds them both with an orb of magical energy and carries them to a chamber deep inside a pyramid. A spiral stairway in the floor curves down deep into the ground.

"We must go down to the molten core of the city," Calculha says. "There will be danger."

"I can take the heat," Wonder Woman replies.

The pair race down the spiral stairs. When they reach the bottom, they enter a large cavern. It is lit by the fiery glow of a lava lake. In the center of the lake is a tall pillar of rock.

"That is where the Leo Crystal once rested," Calculha says.

"Then that is where it will rest once more," Wonder Woman says.

The Amazon leaps over the molten fire and lands on the pillar of rock. It shakes with the force of the earthquake, but Wonder Woman keeps her footing. She sees a spot on the top of the pillar that is carved in the same shape as the Leo Crystal. Wonder Woman leans down and places the Leo Crystal into it. The earthquake stops immediately.

Turn to page 42.

Wonder Woman claps her bracelets together. **CLAAANG!** The powerful shock wave knocks the hunters off their feet. Some fall to the ground. Others stagger off-balance in their heavy armor. Wonder Woman races forward and snatches their energy weapons from their hands. Then she crushes the rifles into a ball.

"Foolish men. I will punish you for attacking me," Morgaine says as she holds out her arms in a gesture of magical power. **FZZZ!** Only a small amount of magical energy flows from her hands. Then it fizzles.

"The Zodiac Crystals drained the magic out of you, remember?" Wonder Woman says. "Let's get out of here."

Wonder Woman leads the way into the jungle, away from the stunned hunters. Morgaine struggles to keep up with the Amazon Princess. The sorceress is not used to being without magic. She cannot fly. She cannot create a spell of protection. She feels weak and helpless, and this makes her angry.

"What is this foul place? It is hot and smells terrible," Morgaine complains loudly. She awkwardly swipes large branches out of her way.

"It's called a jungle," Wonder Woman says as she moves gracefully through the thick tangle of vines and bushes. "Its ecosystem depends on heat and moisture. I'm guessing you don't have much experience with this sort of environment."

Suddenly a small animal bolts across Morgaine's path. The sorceress yelps in surprise.

"Shh! Be very quiet," Wonder Woman warns.

Turn to page 45.

Wonder Woman zooms over the prehistoric landscape. She speeds over lakes and streams, over hills and valleys, and zigzags through the trees of a thick jungle.

The Morgaine monster follows, but even in the form of a mythical hippogriff she can't keep up. Anger boils up in the sorceress. It erupts as blazing magical energy that shoots out of her eyes. Twin beams of raw power streak toward Wonder Woman.

ZZAPOW!

The magical energy strikes the Amazon warrior. The golden lasso wrapped around her waist blazes like the sun. She can feel the Zodiac Crystal surge with power under her belt.

"Back on Earth, Morgaine's magic activated the crystal and it opened a portal," Wonder Woman says to herself. "Maybe I can make it do that again and get us home."

Wonder Woman stops trying to escape from Morgaine le Fey. The Amazon turns and flies straight back at the sorceress.

Turn to page 40.

"I am tired of this cat-and-mouse game. If you want the Zodiac Crystal, Morgaine, you are going to have to fight me for it!" Wonder Woman says.

"That is a challenge I will gladly accept," Morgaine replies as she returns to her human form and glows with magical energy.

ZZABLAM! Morgaine fires a gigantic bolt of magic at Wonder Woman. The Amazon Princess does not try to dodge. She lets it hit her. Beneath her golden lasso, the Zodiac Crystal soaks up the power.

"That tickled. I thought you were a mighty sorceress," Wonder Woman says. She can feel the crystal start to vibrate as its power builds.

Morgaine lets loose with another explosive burst of raw magical energy. She is surprised when this blast is also sucked into Wonder Woman's glowing lasso. But it is not the lasso that is glowing. It is the Zodiac Crystal blazing beneath it. Suddenly a portal opens up.

"What trickery is this?" Morgaine says.

"No trickery, just a way home—I hope," Wonder Woman replies.

Before Morgaine can react, Wonder Woman flies at amazing speed and grabs the sorceress. The Amazon Princess zooms into the energy portal with Morgaine.

They fall through a black void. When they come out, they are in the middle of an alien landscape.

"Well, this isn't Earth," Wonder Woman says as she looks around.

"I don't care where we are. I want that crystal!" Morgaine declares.

"Here we go again," Wonder Woman says and launches into the air.

THE END

To follow another path, turn to page 11.

"Whew! That's a relief," Wonder Woman says.

"Balance has been restored to the Zodiac," Calculha says.

"I'm afraid it might not stay that way for long," Wonder Woman says. "Morgaine le Fey is still out there, and she wants to control all of the Zodiac Crystals. If she steals another one, the destruction will start all over again."

"Do not worry," Calculha says. "I can find her with my magic."

The Master Mage conjures a small globe of energy between his hands. Images take shape on its surface. They show Morgaine blasting huge cracks in the ground as people run for safety.

"Oh no, she's at it again," Wonder Woman says. "I have to stop her. Where is she?"

"Morgaine is in the city of Thamuz," Calculha says. "But rest assured, she will fail to find a Zodiac Crystal."

"How can you be so sure of that?" Wonder Woman asks.

"The Zodiac Crystals rest beneath each of the Twelve Cities on the Zodiac network of magic," Calculha replies. "Thamuz is not one of them."

"She'll figure that out soon enough, but right now she's causing harm and destruction. I have to get to Thamuz—and fast," Wonder Woman says. "But I don't know where Thamuz is."

"I will use my magic to send you there," Calculha says.

"Aren't you coming? Morgaine's sorcery is powerful, but I think your magic can beat hers," Wonder Woman says.

"I must stay and help the people of the City of the Golden Gate," Calculha says. "But I can still help you defeat the sorceress."

Calculha hands Wonder Woman a small amulet.

"This amulet contains a spell of confinement," Calculha says. "Place it on her body and speak her name. That will identify the subject to be confined."

Turn the page.

The Master Mage casts a magical spell of transportation, and instantly Wonder Woman appears in Thamuz. Her arrival catches Morgaine by surprise, and Wonder Woman quickly tags Morgaine with Calculha's amulet.

"Morgaine le Fey," Wonder Woman says.

The amulet glows, and a glowing ball of magic surrounds the sorceress. Morgaine struggles to escape, but she fails.

"It looks like Calculha's magic beats Morgaine's after all," Wonder Woman says.

THE END

To follow another path, turn to page 11.

"Do not silence me!" Morgaine says.

"Be silent if you want to live. We are being hunted," Wonder Woman whispers.

Wonder Woman and Morgaine stand very still. They can hear the sounds of hunters stomping through the jungle. The men shout back and forth to each other, making no effort to be quiet.

"They must be poor hunters if they always make that much noise," Morgaine scoffs.

"They are trying to herd us in a direction they choose," Wonder Woman says.

"They will not succeed," Morgaine declares.

"I like your attitude," Wonder Woman says. "If we work together, we can beat the hunters at their own game."

"I know how to lure a victim into a trap," Morgaine admits.

"Then let's put that knowledge to good use," Wonder Woman says.

Turn the page.

Moments later, the hunters are surprised when they see Morgaine march toward them with Wonder Woman tied up behind her.

"I have captured this prey and declare myself a hunter!" Morgaine says.

Confused, the hunters look at each other.

"Is that even in the rules?" one of them asks.

"You said if I was not prey, I was a hunter," Morgaine says.

"She isn't on the official list," another hunter says as he looks at a small handheld device.

As the others gather around him to view the display, Wonder Woman rises up into the air. She is not tied up after all. The Amazon Princess twirls her golden lasso and snares the hunters with it. She tugs on the lasso and it tightens around them. Then Wonder Woman lifts the hunters off the ground.

"I have captured prey and declare myself a hunter," Wonder Woman says.

Turn to page 48.